Jack Frost's
Ice
Castle

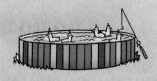

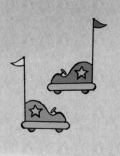

Kylie the Carnival Fairy was originally published
as a Rainbow Magic special. This version has
been specially adapted for developing readers
in conjunction with a Reading Consultant.

Special thanks
to Narinder Dhami
and Fiona Phillipson

Reading Consultant: Prue Goodwin, lecturer in literacy and children's books.

ORCHARD BOOKS

This story first published in Great Britain in 2006 by Orchard Books
First published as an Early Reader in 2012
This edition published in 2019 by The Watts Publishing Group

1 3 5 7 9 10 8 6 4 2

© 2019 Rainbow Magic Limited.
© 2019 HIT Entertainment Limited.
Illustrations © Orchard Books 2012

HiT entertainment

A CIP catalogue record for this book is available from the British Library.

ISBN 978 1 40835 977 8

Printed in China

MIX
Paper from
responsible sources
FSC® C104740

The paper and board used in this book are made from wood from responsible sources

Orchard Books
An imprint of Hachette Children's Group
Part of The Watts Publishing Group Limited
Carmelite House, 50 Victoria Embankment, London EC4Y 0DZ

An Hachette UK Company
www.hachette.co.uk
www.hachettechildrens.co.uk

Kylie
the Carnival Fairy

Daisy Meadows

ORCHARD

www.rainbowmagicbooks.co.uk

The Fairyland Palace

Carnival

Rollercoaster this way

CANDYFLOSS

Sunnyays

GRAND OPENI

COLD DRINKS

Story One

The Hat
Thieves

The Hat
Thieves

It was the holidays and Rachel Walker was visiting her best friend Kirsty Tate. Today it was the grand opening of the Sunnydays Carnival.

"This is so exciting!" said Kirsty. "Look at all the rides!"

"There's the Carnival Master," said Rachel. She pointed to a jolly-looking man in a top hat. He marched up to the gates and threw them open.

"Welcome!" he boomed. "Let the carnival magic begin!"

He pointed at the big wheel with his hat. Slowly the wheel began to turn. The other rides started moving, too.

"It's magic!" gasped a boy.

Rachel and Kirsty smiled. They knew all about magic! The two girls were special friends of the fairies. But spiteful Jack Frost and his goblin servants liked to cause trouble in Fairyland, so Kirsty and Rachel helped the fairies to sort things out.

A loud drum beat echoed

through the air.

"Look at the parade!" Kirsty cried as a band marched by.

A man in a blue and gold peaked cap was leading the parade. He was carrying a rainbow-coloured baton.

Acrobats were cartwheeling along beside the parade. One of them stopped and gave Rachel a party popper.

The girls turned to watch some jugglers. They weren't very good! They kept dropping their balls.

"I think they need a bit more practice," Rachel said.

"They're not very tall," Kirsty noticed. "And they have very long fingernails!" She peered closer and saw that they had long green noses, too. "Rachel!" Kirsty whispered. "Those jugglers are goblins!"

"Why are Jack Frost's goblins here?" Kirsty wondered.

Before Rachel could reply, they saw a goblin dash up to the Carnival Master. The goblin grabbed his hat and ran off. People cheered, because they thought it was part of the show!

Seconds later, more goblins appeared. They rushed towards the Band Leader and soon they had his hat too. He shouted and waved his arms but everyone just laughed.

"We have to put a stop to this!" Rachel told Kirsty.

The band's music suddenly became a horrible din! Then all the rides stopped working at the same time. The Carnival Master waved at the band until they stopped playing.

"The band is having a small problem," he told everyone. "But I'm sure we will sort it out. Don't forget to come to our Closing Day Parade in two days' time. We will crown the best-dressed little boy or girl as Carnival King or Queen!"

The Carnival Master tried

to smile, and a few people cheered.

Rachel and Kirsty suddenly heard hoofbeats. They turned around to see two women in sparkly costumes riding ponies. The women were carrying the beautiful Carnival Crown on top of a blue velvet cushion.

The crowd cheered as
the ponies trotted by. Then
everyone went off to have fun
exploring the carnival.

"I wonder where those
goblins have gone," Rachel
said.

Kirsty began to shiver and
rub her arms. "It's suddenly got
cold," she said.

Rachel stared at a clown in a
baggy yellow costume. "There's
something familiar about him,"
she whispered to Kirsty.

"He's got icicles hanging

from his chin," Kirsty noticed.
"It's Jack Frost!"

Just then, a magical icy wind
swirled around Jack Frost and
carried him into the air. He
landed by the cushion which
carried the Carnival Crown.

He grinned nastily, snatched
the crown and zoomed away.

"Oh no!" cried Rachel.

At that moment her fingers
began to tingle. She looked
down and saw her party
popper burst. A little fairy
shot out of it in a shower
of streamers.

"Hello, girls!" the fairy called.
"I'm Kylie the Carnival Fairy.
I came here to make sure
the Sunnydays Carnival is a
success. But Jack Frost is trying
to spoil everybody's fun!"

The girls looked confused.

Kylie explained the problem.
"The stolen hats are magic,"
she said. "Without the Band
Leader's hat, the music will be
terrible. Without the Carnival
Master's hat, the rides won't
work. The Carnival Crown
is the most important of all.

Without it, the Closing Day Parade will be a mess!"

"We won't let that happen," said Kirsty. "We'll help you find the hats."

Suddenly the girls spotted a goblin's foot disappearing behind a curtain. He was heading for the Log Falls ride!

Rachel and Kirsty followed him as quickly as they could. Two other goblins were with him. One of them had the Carnival Master's hat!

The goblins climbed up to the start of the ride. They got into a boat, which started to move.

"The magic hat is making the ride work," Kylie said.

"I've got an idea," said Rachel. "If we just wait here, the goblins will float past us. Then we can grab the hat!"

The log boat shot down a slide towards the girls. In the back of the boat, a goblin sat holding the hat. Kirsty leaned over and snatched it!

"Perfect!" laughed Kylie.

The goblins shouted angrily. Kirsty and Rachel ignored them and ran off towards the Carnival Master's tent.

The worried Carnival Master was talking to the Band Leader.

"I don't understand why the rides don't work!" he said. "I must go and help to fix them!"

While he was away, the girls sneaked inside and put the hat back on his desk.

"My hat!" cried the Carnival Master when he came back.

"How did it get here?"

He put the hat back on and went to show it to the Band Leader. All the rides started working again.

Kirsty and Rachel smiled.

"Thank you both so much," said Kylie happily. "Now I must go back to Fairyland and tell everyone the good news."

The girls waved to the fairy until she vanished in a shower of sparkles.

"Now people can enjoy the rides," said Kirsty. "But what about the music?"

"We won't let Jack Frost spoil the carnival," Rachel said. "We'll look for the Band Leader's hat next!"

Story Two

Magical
Music

Magical
Music

It was the day after the
grand opening, and Rachel
and Kirsty were back at the
Sunnydays Carnival.

"What's that terrible noise?"
Rachel asked. She clapped her
hands over her ears.

"It's the band," Kirsty said.
"Their music is going wrong
because the Band Leader's hat
is missing!"

People were frowning at the
band and sticking their fingers
into their ears. The Band
Leader looked miserable.

The Carnival Master ran
onto the stage, looking upset.

"I really don't know what's going on!" he said. He waved the musicians off the stage.

Kirsty and Rachel watched sadly as the gloomy musicians went back to their tent.

"We've got to find the Band Leader's hat," Rachel said.

The girls wandered around the carnival for a while. They passed a candy-floss stall and a face-painting tent.

"Oh, there's a hall of mirrors," said Rachel. "I love funny mirrors! Let's go in."

Kirsty swung the door open and stepped inside. For a second everything was dark, but then the lights came on. The tall mirrors showed hundreds of reflections of Kirsty and Rachel.

"This is weird," Rachel laughed.

Suddenly there was a burst of sparkly glitter.

"Where did that come from?" Kirsty gasped.

The mirrors around them showed hundreds of reflections of a colourful little fairy.

"It's Kylie!" said Rachel.

"I'm so glad to see you,"
Kylie said. "I can sense that the
Band Leader's hat is nearby!"

"Come with us and help us
look for it," said Kirsty. "Let's
search in the fancy dress tent!"

At the tent, some cub scouts were having their faces painted. One of them was wearing a witch costume. But there were no carnival people around.

"The scouts are painting each other's faces," said Kirsty. "Why aren't carnival people doing it?

Rachel turned to look too. She saw the scout in the witch costume sit on a chair and pull off his hat.

"You paint my face now!" shouted the scout in the witch costume. "It's my turn!"

The other scout had tiger stripes painted on his face. But when the girls looked closely they saw that both boys had long noses and green skin!

"They're goblins!" Kirsty said.

"And they've got the Band Leader's hat!" said Rachel. She had spotted it lying on a table inside the tent.

"If Kylie changes us into fairies we can fly in and get the hat," Kirsty said.

Kylie waved her wand to make the girls fairy-sized. Then all three of them flew into the tent. Before they reached the table, the goblin with the tiger stripes grabbed the Band Leader's hat. He jammed it onto his head, then ran outside.

"Hey, where are you going?" the goblin in the witch costume shouted.

The stripy-faced goblin stuck out his tongue. "I'm going to have some fun on the rides!" he shouted back.

"After him!" said Kirsty.

The three friends flew after
the stripy-faced goblin as he
ran towards a teacup ride.

"I want to have fun, too!"
cried the witch goblin. He ran
towards the ride as well.

The goblins jumped into a teacup and the ride started up.

"I've got an idea," said Rachel. "Kylie, can you turn us back to human-size? Then make the ride spin really fast."

"Of course!" said the little fairy. Her eyes twinkled.

The goblins were enjoying themselves as their teacup began to turn. "WHEE!" they shouted, and waved their arms.

Kylie pointed her wand and sent sparkling fairy dust rushing towards the ride. The teacup began to spin faster and faster.

"I feel sick," one of the goblins groaned. "Somebody switch this thing off!"

The goblins turned even greener than usual.

The ride spun even faster!

The goblin wearing the
Band Leader's hat put up a
hand to hold it firmly on his
head. But he was too late.
The hat flew off and tumbled
through the air.

"My hat!" he shrieked.

Rachel hurried over and picked it up.

Kylie waved her wand again and the teacup stopped spinning. The goblins climbed out. They had to lie down because they were too dizzy to walk.

"Quickly!" Kylie said to Kirsty and Rachel. "If we hurry we can get the hat back to the Band Leader in time for the afternoon show!"

The girls rushed to the tent next to the stage and peeped inside. It was full of musicians.

"How can we give the hat to the Band Leader without being seen?" Kirsty asked.

"Let go of the hat and I'll use magic to put it on the Band Leader's desk!" Kylie said.

Rachel let go of the hat.

Kylie shrank it to fairy-size with a flick of her wand. Then she sent it whizzing over to the desk.

The hat landed next to the Band Leader's baton. With a puff of fairy magic it grew back to its normal size.

When the Band Leader came over to collect his baton, he couldn't believe his eyes.

"My hat!" he cried. "Where on earth could it have been?"

"Never mind now," said the Carnival Master. "It's time for

the afternoon show. The band have had a break, so maybe they'll be able to play better this time."

The Band Leader nodded. Kirsty and Rachel shared a smile. The band certainly were going to play better, and they knew exactly why!

The Band Leader proudly placed the hat on his head.

"We'll make this our best performance ever," he said.

The musicians started playing a lovely tune. They marched smartly out of the tent. Soon everyone was watching them and cheering.

"Phew! Everything's back to normal!" Rachel said.

"Not quite," Kylie said. "Don't forget that those naughty goblins have still got the Carnival Crown."

"Don't worry, Kylie," Kirsty said. "We'll do our best to find the crown."

Rachel and Kirsty stood back and watched as the band paraded all the way around the carnival grounds.

"Thank you again for your help!" Kylie smiled gratefully.

"Now go and enjoy yourselves. I will return to Fairyland and tell everyone the news."

"See you tomorrow!" Kirsty smiled and waved.

Then the two girls ran off to the roller-coaster. It was time for them to have some well-earned fun!

Story Three

The Carnival Crown

The Carnival Crown

It was the last evening of
the Sunnydays Carnival.
Everyone was wearing fancy
dress. Rachel and Kirsty were
wearing black cat costumes.
Kirsty's parents were dressed
as colourful clowns.

"There's a hook-a-duck game!" cried Rachel. She pointed to a stall where some plastic ducks were bobbing around in a tub of water.

"Can we have a go?" Kirsty asked her mum.

"Of course," said Mrs Tate. "We'll meet you at the fireworks display later."

Rachel picked up a fishing rod and tried to hook a duck. She did it! Then she heard a tiny voice say, "Hello, Rachel!"

The girls peered down at the

duck Rachel had hooked.
Kylie was sitting on its back!

"I'm glad to see you," said
the fairy. "But I have some bad
news. Jack Frost doesn't think
the goblins have been causing
enough mischief on their own.

So he's come to help them!"

"Have you seen any goblins yet, Kylie?" Rachel asked.

Kylie didn't reply. Instead she pointed at three boys in jesters' costumes. They were running towards the Tunnel of Love ride. They all had green faces!

"They're goblins!" said Kirsty. "Let's follow them."

The girls hurried into the ride. The goblins were sitting in a carriage at the front of the train. Rachel and Kirsty sat near the back and hoped the goblins wouldn't see them.

The train set off into the tunnel. It drove past lots of pretty painted scenes. Then it slowed down beside a plastic tree. The goblins got off.

Kirsty, Rachel and Kylie jumped out of their carriage, too. They hid behind the tree and listened.

"Hurry up, you idiots!" shouted a grumpy voice. The girls peeped around the tree and saw Jack Frost sitting on a throne of ice!

"He's wearing the Carnival Crown!" whispered Kirsty.

Jack Frost glared at his goblins. "You're having too much fun!" he said. "You should be spoiling the carnival for the humans. Stop enjoying yourselves and get on with your jobs!"

"Let's sneak up to the throne and grab the crown!" Rachel said. The girls and Kylie began to creep up behind Jack Frost.

The goblins were talking about all the naughty things they were going to do.

"I'll steal all the toffee apples and eat them!" said one goblin.

"I'll scare the children with spooky noises!" said another.

"That's a good idea," Jack Frost said. "Now go and do it!"

The goblins went to obey him.

Rachel saw the crown poking over the back of the icy throne. She tried to grab it, but Jack Frost stood up quickly and turned around.

"You can't fool me!" he sneered. "I knew you were there all the time."

"Please give us back the Carnival Crown!" said Kylie.

But Jack Frost just laughed and jumped into the train.

He waved as it drove off.

The girls rushed outside to look for him.

"He must have passed by the Log Falls," said Kirsty. "Look, the water is all frozen!"

Rachel spotted Jack Frost getting onto the big wheel.

"He can't freeze the big wheel, can he?" asked Kirsty.

"He might try," Kylie said. "We have to stop him."

Kirsty and Rachel jumped into the seat behind Jack Frost.

"If only we could get to the crown," said Kirsty. "But we can't reach it from here."

"I've got an idea!" said Rachel. "Kylie, can you magic up a fishing rod with a hook on the end? Then we can hook the crown!"

"Just like the hook-a-duck game!" Kirsty said.

Kylie fluttered into the air and waved her wand. There was a burst of sparkles and a shiny gold fishing rod appeared in Rachel's hands.

"Perfect," she said.

The girls waited until their seats went over the top of the big wheel. Now Jack Frost was below them. Rachel held out the rod. Kylie fluttered down and slipped the hook through one of the holes in the crown.

Jack Frost didn't notice the crown being lifted off his head. He was too busy enjoying the view from the big wheel. But when the ride ended, he put his hand on top of his head.

"Where's my crown?" Jack
Frost yelled.

The girls had just got off the
ride. They ran away but Kirsty
tripped. The crown shot out
of her hands and flew towards
the stage. Jack Frost caught it
before it could land.

"Oh, no!" Rachel cried.

Suddenly, a spotlight came on. Everyone looked at Jack Frost!

The Carnival Master rushed onto the stage and shook Jack Frost's hand. "You've found the Carnival Crown!" he cried. "Thank you so much!"

"That's a wonderful costume!" the Band Leader told Jack Frost.

"Er, yes," Jack Frost agreed.

"Please help me announce the winner of the costume competition," the Carnival Master said.

Jack Frost was starting to look pleased by all the attention. The Carnival Master gave him a piece of paper. Jack Frost read out: "This year's Carnival Queen is Alexandra Kirby!"

Everyone clapped as a little girl in a princess costume climbed onto the stage.

"He'll have to give her

the crown," said Rachel. "He can't steal it again with all these people watching!"

For a moment Jack Frost looked like he might run away. Then he shoved the crown into the Carnival Master's hands.

"The crown is safe!" said Kylie. "Thank you so much, girls! Now you'd better hurry back to Kirsty's parents."

The girls said goodbye to Kylie. They ran across the field to meet Mr and Mrs Tate just as the fireworks display began.

"Those are the best fireworks
I've ever seen," said Mr Tate.

Rachel and Kirsty grinned
at each other. They knew
that fairy magic was adding
extra-special sparkle to the
Sunnydays Carnival!

**If you enjoyed this story,
you may want to read**

Florence the
Friendship Fairy
Early Reader

Here's how the story begins…

Rachel Walker was staying
with her best friend Kirsty Tate.
One day they looked through
Kirsty's scrapbook, which was
full of lovely things.

Kirsty and Rachel had a
special secret. They were friends
with the fairies! The scrapbook
reminded them of all the fun

they had enjoyed together.

"I hope we'll have another fairy adventure soon," Kirsty whispered.

Then she frowned.

"There's an empty space here. I don't remember that," she said.

Worse still, when Rachel

turned the next page she saw
that one photo was damaged.
Another one looked unfamiliar.

"I don't recognise her," said
Rachel. She pointed to a
picture of a pretty fairy.

Before either girl could say
another word, the fairy began
to sparkle. She flew straight out

from the page!

"I'm Florence the Friendship Fairy," she said. "My magical memory book protects people's special memories."

"How lovely," said Kirsty. "But I don't think the magic is working at the moment."

Rachel held up the damaged scrapbook, and Florence looked at it sadly...

Read
Florence the Friendship Fairy
Early Reader
to find out
what happens next!

Discover the world of

RAINBOW magic™

- ❤ There are over 130 Rainbow Magic fairies for you to meet

- ❤ Perfect for newly confident readers

- ❤ Great for reading aloud

- ❤ Each book makes reading fun. Remember to enjoy the experience together!

- ❤ Over 27 million copies sold!

Everybody loves Daisy Meadows!

'I love your books' – Jasmine, Essex

'You are my favourite author' – Aimee, Surrey

'I am a big fan of Rainbow Magic!' – Emma, Hertfordshire

Meet the first seven
Rainbow Fairies

Ruby
the Red Fairy

Amber
the Orange Fairy

Saffron
the Yellow Fairy

Fern
the Green Fairy

Sky
the Blue Fairy

Izzy
the Indigo Fairy

Heather
the Violet Fairy

Become a
Rainbow Magic
fairy friend and be the first to
see sneak peeks of new books.

There are lots of special offers and exclusive
competitions to win sparkly
Rainbow Magic prizes.

Sign up today at
www.rainbowmagicbooks.co.uk